CINDERELLA

ON THE

BALL

Attic Press

Dublin

First Published in 1991 by
Attic Press
4 Upper Mount Street
Dublin 2

British Library Cataloguing in Publication Data

Cinderella On The Ball - (Feminist fairytales)
  1. Fairbairns, Zoë 11. Series
  823.01089287 (FS)

  ISBN 18559402726-4

Cover Design: Denise Kierans
Origination: Attic Press
Printing: The Guernsey Press Company Ltd.

CONTENTS

Damsel in Distress

ONCE, LONG AGO, there lived a young girl named Damsel. Although pretty and reaching her prime she was not yet betrothed, as few visitors came to the fortress in which she lived. One sunny day, however, Damsel was picking flowers in the meadows when who should ride by but the famous knight, Sir Gallant. Dressed in shining armour and sitting high on his fearless steed, Sir Gallant lost his heart to Damsel and pledged his love forthwith. 'I will make you a lady the like of which the world has not yet known', he swore, and so Damsel went to live with him in his castle far away.

The first months were filled with happiness. Everything Damsel wished for was hers, though in truth she asked for little but his love. They wined and dined their neighbours and the castle became famous for its hospitality. 'You are the most beautiful and talented hostess in the world,' Sir Gallant proudly told his lady, and the townspeople cheered her name, grateful for the prosperity she had brought them. But soon a cloud grew ominously from the east and whispers of war in distant lands reached their castle home.

'I must leave you to lead a Crusade, for my honour is at stake,' Sir Gallant told Damsel, and her heart grew heavy as she thought of the days and nights she would have to spend alone. 'Please do not leave me by myself,' she begged him, 'for I am nothing without you.' But he was not swayed. 'Fear not, for I shall return, my love, and when the Crusade is finished we shall have all the time in the world to spend together,' and he rode away on his brave horse into the raging east.

Day followed night and night followed day. Poor Damsel wept alone into countless handkerchiefs. She neither ate nor slept, and rarely saw the flowers in the meadows or the ripening buds upon the trees. However, one morning as the sun rose, Damsel saw light glinting in the east and, with a great bursting of joy in her heart, recognised Sir Gallant's return from afar. She ran to meet him and was soon listening to his heroic adventures in distant lands.

As the weeks sped by the castle once again echoed with song and laughter, and the famous knight watched his lady blossom with love. The harvest ripened and there was much merry-making, and Damsel forgot about the months spent in wretched loneliness and tears. She listened enrapt as Sir Gallant told her of all the things they would accomplish together, and smiled as she thought of their future. But as the leaves withered and began to fall, once more clouds gathered and rumours of war began to spread. With doom dragging at her heart, Damsel begged Sir Gallant to stay with her and not lead the coming Crusade. 'All I ask of you is your love,' she told him, 'and for you to stay with me, for without you I am nothing.' But he would not heed her words.

'My honour is at stake,' he answered. 'It is my duty! But when the fighting is over we shall have all the time in the world to spend together.' Tears ran down her face as, once again, Damsel watched her love depart into the east.

The weeks dragged by and the weather grew cold. But Damsel hardly noticed this for she kept to her room, with her red-rimmed eyes, hardly eating and barely sleeping.

'We shall all starve if Sir Gallant does not return soon!' said the townspeople. 'For Lady Damsel has bought neither food nor clothing from us since he went away.' The only traders invited to the castle were linen merchants. 'And we simply cannot keep up with the demand for handkerchiefs,' they told the others worriedly. However, soon the crusading knight returned to save them all from starvation, and once again Damsel ran joyously to meet him. She forgot the days and nights spent alone and, as hardly a week went by without a banquet at the castle, the traders once more found a market for their wares.

'You are by far the fairest and cleverest of ladies,' Sir Gallant told his ladylove as they waved another party of guests farewell. 'You have my heart and I shall never leave you!' he swore. Damsel almost burst with joy as she listened to his words, and believed him.

Christmas brought snow. They huddled by the fire, Sir Gallant entrancing her with stories of the east, of blood-drenched fields, of battles lost and won, and honour restored. The March winds blew and suddenly spring had arrived. Damsel ran to pick daffodils in the meadows and so was the first to see the company of armoured men making for the castle. Her heart almost stopped beating as dread coursed through her body and she hurried to the courtyard.

Sir Gallant was standing by his horse conversing with the soldiers. One look at her knight, once more dressed in armour, sent Damsel running to the cloister where she wept bitterly. At last he came to her. 'Do not distress yourself, my love, for war is nigh and it is my duty to lead the Crusade,' he told her. 'But when it is over we shall have all the time in the world to spend together.'

'But you swore you would never leave me again,' she cried, 'and I am but nothing without you beside me!'

He turned to her. 'You know, fair lady, that I love you above all others, but I beg you do not try to hold me back, for my honour is at stake.' She could not speak as he took his leave. 'Damsel, I shall return I know not when. Pray keep busy and the time will pass quickly.' He kissed her hand as he made his departure.

The first day dragged by and the linen merchants got busy with their handkerchief making. Damsel thought bitterly of Sir Gallant's broken promise and parting words to her. She thought sorrowfully of her beloved knight engaged in countless heroic deeds far away and, suddenly, a thought assailed her. What better way to keep busy than to weave her own tapestry, each inch depicting Sir Gallant's brave deeds? Enlivened with sudden energy Damsel rushed to her loom in the turret, ordering her page to bring yarns of all the colours of the rainbow.

And so began the tapestry. Day and night she worked, hardly stopping to eat or sleep, and it seemed as though her knight stood beside her once again as she wove his stories into the fabric. The spinners, too, worked night and day to keep up with her demand for the coloured yarns, and at last the tapestry was almost complete. Damsel, so engrossed in her work, hardly noticed the added bustle going on about her. 'He has returned, my lady!' the page told her. 'Sir Gallant is home!' '

'Tell him I shall be down to greet him soon,' Damsel told the boy and she turned to finish the last corner of her masterpiece.

The door was suddenly thrust open behind her and, in a moment, Sir Gallant stood beside his lady. 'Welcome home, my love', she said, her fingers engaged in the weaving. '

'Why did you not come to meet me?' he asked her, surprised. 'You know my return is worth nothing without you beside me!'

'Forgive me, Sir Gallant, I have just this last corner to complete. But when my tapestry is finished we shall have all the time in the world to spend together,' she explained, continuing with her work, and sent him downstairs until she was ready.

All that summer Damsel's tapestry hung upon the wall in the dining hall. Their visitors admired it and it became much talked about. People travelled from far and wide to view it and, when the autumn arrived and once more a Crusade was arranged, Damsel had been commissioned to work upon another tapestry for a rich neighbour.

'Farewell, my lovely. Once more I go to do my duty,' Sir Gallant told her again, but this time Damsel did not beg him to stay. Her mind, indeed, was more on the design of the weave of her new tapestry than on his departure and when her brave knight rode from the castle, she ran upstairs to her loom and began her work feverishly. The tapestry was finished and Damsel was half-way through another commission when her crusader returned to the castle. 'He has returned, my lady', the page told her, arriving in the turret laden with yarns.

'Pray, tell Sir Gallant that I am busy, but when I have finished this corner I shall be there to greet him,' she answered, her mind on the yarn to choose for the colour of the primrose pattern. Hours passed and still Damsel worked at her loom. Finally, Sir Gallant, battle-tired and weary, climbed the steep stairs to attend her.

'I am home, Damsel!' he told her. 'Why did you not come to greet me?'

'Forgive me, my love. My mind was engrossed on this work,' she replied.

'Pray, leave your loom and come to me, for my life has no meaning without you beside me,' he pleaded.

'I am sorry, but it is my duty,' she told him. 'I have to finish this commission, for my honour is at stake. But do not worry, Sir Gallant, for when this tapestry is finished we shall have all the time in the world to spend together.'

And so the winter months passed by. The Christmas guests were amazed at Damsel's artistic talents and more commissions flowed in. Now, part of every day was devoted to her loom and poor Sir Gallant felt lost without her.

'You have changed, my lovely,' he told her sadly. 'I no longer mean so much to you.'

'It's simply that I am busy with my weaving, but I do love you still, Sir Gallant,' she assured him, climbing the stairs once more to her loom.

The spring sunshine brought news of another war. Damsel hardly noticed her knight's departure, so engrossed was she in her work. The weeks rushed by and more finished tapestries left the castle for their new owners. Summer came and with it a make-shift carriage, bearing the wounded body of Sir Gallant, bloodied and barely breathing.

'Where is my love? Where is Damsel?' he cried and the page ran to the weaving room in the turret to tell Damsel the sad news.

'I am sorry, I cannot leave my loom just now,' she answered. 'But when I have finished this tapestry I shall go to Sir Gallant and we shall have all the time in the world to spend together.'

When Sir Gallant was told her words he begged the page to entreat her to come to him. 'I cannot bear this pain much longer. I need my love beside me, for without her I am nothing!' he cried in anguish. But Damsel told the page, 'Pray, tell Sir Gallant that I must finish my tapestry, for it is my duty and my honour is at stake!' And she turned back to her commission, frowning, for she could not decide on a scene to weave into the top-most corner.

Some time later the page returned. 'Sir Gallant has breathed his last, my lady', he told her sadly. For a moment Damsel was silent. Then she jumped quickly from her chair by the loom. 'I entreat you, do not move my brave Knight's body, for this is just the picture I need to complete my tapestry!' And the page ran from the room to carry out her order.

Damsel took a sheaf of yarns from the rack and quickly hurried downstairs to the courtyard where the make-shift carriage bearing Sir Gallant awaited her. There she knelt by the body of her lost love and carefully studied it, for she wished to match the exact colour of his blood with the spinners' yarns so that she could weave the scene into her tapestry.

Margaret Neylon

The Princess and the Sun

ONCE UPON A time, an old king dwelt in a dismal country to the north of everywhere. He had been so long in his kingdom, he could not remember how he came to be there. A curse was upon him and his land. That was all he knew. The sun never shone there and it was always dark. Night never slipped into day but was always night, so there was nothing to pluck at his memory of what was or what could be. It was as if the past had never existed and a future was unthinkable.

And in this eternal night no laughter was ever heard. Neither the king nor his subjects laughed at anything. And looking round it was easy to understand why. The kingdom was barren: the ground was infertile and what remained of trees were but stunted growths. And because the sun never shone, there were no seasons in this grim world. Winter never turned to spring and children grew up without ever knowing summer. For this was the Land Of Never.

But one morning something stirred. The king was restless and as he heard his three sons approaching he rose up quickly to greet them. In the dim artificial light his rheumy eyes fell on them: on Roland, the eldest, handsome and spiteful, on Cedric, his second son, ill-mannered and a bully, and lastly on his youngest son, Michael. As Michael came towards him, the king felt his heart beat a little faster. For him a flicker of love remained. There was little love in this dark land and what there was remained hidden, for in the Land of Always Night love was seen as a weakness.

As the king looked at Michael he remembered why he was feeling restless. The previous night, if you could call it night, he had had a dream. And now as it came back to him he began to speak.

'My sons, last night I had a dream.'

Michael looked at his father with interest while Cedric raised his eyebrows in derision and Roland smirked.

'I dreamt,' the king continued, 'that in a far-off kingdom there lives a princess who can lift the curse from our land. She lives in the Land of Always and I want one of you to go there and bring her here.'

'But,' asked Michael, 'what woman would want to come and live in a place like this?'

This brought a loud guffaw from Cedric.

'What woman would want!' he repeated. 'Any woman *I* want will do what I tell her.' Roland nodded at his brother.

The king would have liked to send Michael to the Land of Always but he knew he had to send his eldest son Roland. He turned to him now, 'You will take my white horse with you. No woman can ever resist a white horse and once she is on it my horse will return to me.'

And after giving him more instructions the king went back into his chambers and there he opened a small casket and unfolded a piece of worn parchment on which these words were written:

From another land a princess torn,
from women's tears a Sun is born.

Was the riddle going to be solved at last and his kingdom set free from the curse, the king wondered, as he watched his son set out on his journey.

Over days and nights Roland travelled across forests and mountains, oceans and seas, orchards and woodlands until at last he arrived at a land where it was always day. The prince blinked in the daylight and found it hard to keep his eyes open but his horse was sure of foot and finally put him down beside a stream. As Roland had never seen running water before he stared at it in amazement. The horse began to drink and suddenly a huge green frog jumped out of the water.

The frog addressed the prince politely but Roland who was very proud answered angrily. 'How dare you speak to me, Prince Roland of Never. Get out of my sight.' And he lifted his boot to kick it but the frog leapt away just in time.

Then Roland got back on the horse again and they did not stop until they came to the gates of a palace. The gates opened as they approached, and there in the garden filled with flowers of every colour and description was a beautiful young princess bent over a flower-bed, watering it from a beautiful golden watering-can. Roland could not see her face properly but from what he could see and from her beautiful golden curls he knew this was the princess. He went over and introduced himself.

The princess answered in the sweetest voice he had ever heard but she did not look up from her work. Then Roland remembered what his father had told him and he led the white horse to her. As he did the horse whinnied loudly and a woman came running out of the palace. It was the princess's sister. 'Who is making all this noise? she demanded. And then she saw the white horse. And before Roland could do anything she had jumped on its back and the horse was on its way to the Land of Never.

When they arrived the king knew this was not the princess in his dream and so he sent his second son Cedric to the Land of Always. But Cedric fared no better. Arriving in the land where it was always day he too met the frog and threatened to turn him into a purse for his troubles. He too saw the princess at work with her flowers but as soon as he led the white horse to her it neighed loudly and the princess's other sister came running out of the palace and soon she too was on her way to the Land of Never.

When she got there she found her sister crying: that is all she had done since she'd realised where she was. And her sister joined in and their wailing could be heard all over the kingdom.

So now the king sent his youngest son Michael and told him not to fail. And when Michael arrived in the land where it was always day his eyes widened in delight at what he saw. And when he came to the running stream the same green frog appeared and Michael smiled at it. And when the frog asked him why he was there Michael told him. He also told him how he feared the princess would never leave such a beautiful place. But the frog told him not to be deceived by the beauty of the land: that to live where it was always day had its own problems. And then he gave Michael some advice.

Michael arrived at the garden gates and there in the garden he saw the princess. She was planting seeds and her head was bent over her work. Michael followed the frog's advice. He went and knelt down beside her and spoke gently to her and looked her straight in the face. And the princess turned to him and Michael saw that she was blind and could not see him. And he understood why his brothers had failed. And he was glad. For as he looked at her his heart melted with love and he could not bear to have tricked her.

And the princess heard the sad note in his voice and touching his face felt a warm tear. She asked him what was wrong. And he told her about his father's dream, adding that he could never ask her to come to the land where he lived, away from all the light and beauty that surrounded her. But the princess laughed a silvery laugh: 'Light and beauty are inside us and we can take them wherever we go. I will come to your kingdom.'

And putting what remained of her seeds in her pocket and holding tightly to her golden watering-can she mounted the white horse and the two of them set off for the Land of Never. And as they travelled further and further north the princess felt the cold winds upon her cheeks, and the icicles brushing her eyelashes. And she heard the piercing cries of lost birds across the snowy wastes.

But the first sound they heard when they reached the Land of Never was the wailing of her two sisters. The princess ran to comfort them but they wouldn't let her, blaming her instead for their predicament. So the princess left them and went for a walk in the palace grounds and she felt the gloom and the darkness of the place seep into her and her courage began to desert her. To distract her thoughts she bent down and tried to plant a seed but the earth was too hard and as she knelt there tears sprang to her eyes and ran down her cheeks and formed a little pool in the hard ground. And the ground softened and the princess was able to plant her seeds.

And every night and, since it was always night, every day the princess gathered her sisters' tears and watered her seeds. And as the dark days went by the sisters cried more and more and the princess was kept very busy watering her plants. At last a little shoot pushed its way up through the ground. The princess danced for joy and brought Michael to see it. He didn't like to tell her it was a weak-looking thing and so he kept quiet. But he was worried. The plant continued to grow, the stem getting longer and longer, but no flower or fruit appeared on it. And even the king began to lose hope. How was the princess going to lift the curse from his kingdom?

Then one day, or was it night, one of the king's servants came running into his room. 'I've seen the sun,' he shouted, waving his arms and forgetting to bow to the king in his excitement.

The king followed the servant into the garden and there indeed on top of the long spindly stem the princess had planted, sat a bright yellow sun. The king fell down and kissed the earth, and other people came running, for the servant had gone and shouted it in the village, and when they saw the golden orb they too fell down and kissed the ground.

The princess heard the commotion and came out and walked slowly over to her plant. As she raised her hand and touched the delicate petals of the sunflower her face broke into a radiant smile. And the people began to laugh and cry and fling their arms round one another. For they had never seen the earth produce before.

Then the king spoke and asked if anyone knew why they had been cursed or why the earth was infertile. At first no one answered. Then an old woman came forward. 'The curse was on your father's father,' she said. 'For he was a warlike man with no respect for the land other than to grab it for himself. And he waged war after war to get more land. At last all the other kingdoms united against him, but rather than let them have his land he despoiled it so that nothing could grow on it. And the skies darkened that day with blood and a curse was put upon this land and on all your grandfather's children until ...' And she stopped speaking, for everyone's eyes were turned to the sky where an opening was perceived. And then there was a blueness and the sun appeared. And the petals of the sunflower slowly uncurled and the people knew the curse had been lifted.

And they turned to the princess to thank her and suddenly they felt sorry she could neither see the sun nor the sunflower and when they spoke their voices were filled with sadness. But the princess knew their thoughts and said: 'People with sight are often blinded by the world, so take care to nourish what is in your hearts and not only what is in front of your eyes.' And the people took her words into their hearts and tried to live happily ever after.

Moya Roddy

The Ugly Sisters Strike Back

ONCE UPON A time, there were two sisters who lived in a kingdom far far away. It was doubtful if either of them would ever have won a beauty contest, since they did not even try to conform to the currently accepted image of female pulchritude. In fact, they were regarded as being somewhat eccentric, because they were both quite content to look like themselves.

One day, their mother announced that their stepsister, called Cinderella, was coming to live with them. The recent death of the sisters' estranged father had left the poor girl all alone in the world.

Now the sisters had every intention of welcoming their younger stepsister with open arms. But they were horrified to discover that she was a frivolous, simpering creature, who had been terribly spoilt because she was considered so pretty and dainty. As a result, she believed that it was her right to be feted and indulged. 'You're *ugly*,' she told the two sisters. 'From now on, I'm going to call you the Ugly Sisters!' And she gave one of her well-practised tinkling laughs, which she thought delightful, but which grated endlessly on her stepsisters' nerves.

While the two sisters were studying law and politics respectively, Cinderella didn't want to do anything but paint her face, practise seductive poses in front of the mirror, and admire her own reflection. 'You'll never get a man!' she used to sneer at them. 'What's the use of all that studying? Surely you know that men don't like women to be cleverer than *they* are.' But the sisters merely smiled and got on with their studies, each earning a first class honours degree later that year.

At precisely the same time, the king of the land announced that he was about to retire. However, he was concerned that his son, who was to succeed him, was 'a bit of a lad', and much given to hanging around ale-houses and other places of ill-repute. He had the idea that perhaps a good woman would be the makings of his son, so he planned a great ball, to which all the young ladies of the land were invited.

'Sounds a bit like a cattle market,' remarked one of the sisters as she opened her invitation. The other sister agreed, but said, 'Let's go, anyway. They can keep their toy-boy prince, but who knows what other interesting people we might meet? Besides, I've always wanted to have a look around the palace, to see for myself if the rumours about the king's greed are true. It's often said that he spends far too much of tax-payers' money on himself, and not enough on services for his subjects.'

'Good idea,' replied her sister. 'My own studies have got me interested in alternative political systems, and have caused me to seriously question the benefits of living under a monarchy.'

Of course Cinderella was thrilled at the idea of attending the ball and at the possibility of snaring a prince. She had finally found a focus for all her wiggles and pouts, which she now practised with renewed vigour before the mirror each day, boring her stepsisters silly with her endless chatter about what she was going to wear on the night. 'If I hear any more talk about her dress, her diet or the pre-menstrual pimple that's appeared on her chin, I'll throttle her,' one of the sisters remarked darkly to the other. In fact, the sisters themselves decided to wear their jeans to the ball, regarding it as more important to be comfortable, rather than opting for the hassle and self-preoccupation involved in wearing some outlandish creation.

On the night of the ball, Cinderella did indeed look a pretty sight, as long as she didn't stretch, move about or blink too often, that is. Her all-over tan and blushing cheekbones had taken a litre of make-up and several hours to apply. And her false eyelashes, which caused a minor hurricane each time she blinked, were a feat of engineering, patience and defiance of gravity. Her skimpy dress was so tight and her shoes were so high that she could hardly walk. Thus constrained, she was unable to stroll to the palace at a leisurely pace with her stepsisters. Instead, she had to wait for a number 45 bus, then almost lost her already precarious balance and laddered her tights as the bus started off.

At the palace, the ball was already in full swing when Cinderella arrived. The floor was crowded with lots of young painted and powdered hopefuls, all of whom were doing their level best to catch the prince's eye. But as soon as Cinderella minced in ('walk' would be an inappropriate word here since she couldn't) the prince had eyes for no one else. It seemed as if all her carefully-studied techniques had paid off, and in gleeful spite, when the price wasn't looking, she dug her stiletto heel into a nearby rival's foot.

However Cinderella's stepsisters weren't exactly idle at the ball either. They were, in fact, chatting up a number of attractive, articulate and influential ministers, who shared not only their political and social views, but also their disquiet over the existing political situation in the land.

Just as midnight approached, one of Cinderella's carefully glued-on false eyelashes came unstuck. With it dangling from one side of her eye like a demented spider she rushed to the cloakroom before the prince could discover that the attributes he so much admired were not entirely natural. As the clock struck midnight, she was still incarcerated in the cloakroom because as she attempted to lever the false eyelash back into place, several of her false nails dropped off, and fell, irretrievably, down the plughole in the sink. As she broke out in a sweat, her carefully-applied suntan began to trickle in streaks down her body...

In embarrassment and desperation, Cinderella rushed from the cloakroom and out through the palace door. There was only one option available to her now - to get home as quickly as she could. Under no circumstances could she let the prince see her looking so disastrously unlike the natural beauty he thought her to be.

Teetering down the palace steps, it was inevitable that Cinderella was going to come a cropper. And she did, somersaulting head over stiletto heels down the stairway, and breaking an ankle that swelled so quickly that her shoe would no longer fit it. So she left it there on the steps, and before anyone could witness her further humiliation, she hobbled as best she could to the casualty department of the nearest hospital.

In vain, the prince now searched for Cinderella with whom he had fallen deeply in love. Gone was his desire to hang around ale-houses and massage parlours. Instead, all he wanted to do was hang around Cinderella. Just before she had inexplicably rushed off to the cloakroom, he had been on the point of asking her to marry him, so that he could gaze forever more at those beautiful eyelashes, that lovely glowing face, and hold forever more those hands with such beautiful and perfect fingernails ...

Disconsolate now, the prince searched everywhere for his 'natural' beauty. Finding her shoe on the palace steps, he vowed to find the owner and marry her forthwith. So with shoe in hand, he set off to search the entire kingdom. Everywhere he went, young females did their best to stuff their foot into the shoe, but all to no avail. Cinderella seemed to have disappeared into thin air.

One day, the prince came to the hospital where Cinderella was incarcerated. But while she recognised *him*, he did not recognise *her*. For without her painted cheeks, fake tan, false eyelashes and fingernails, she looked completely different. (In fact, she looked much healthier and prettier without all the artifice that she usually employed.) However, her vanity would not allow her to reveal her true identity, so as the prince walked through the ward, she stifled a sob and buried her face in the pillow.

The sad prince returned alone to the palace, only to discover that there had been a peaceful revolution in his absence. His father had been moved to a rest home for elderly kings, and gone from the palace were all the priceless paintings, tapestries and books. They had been placed in art galleries and libraries, where the entire population could now enjoy them. In place of the old order, a new political system, based on liberty and equality for all, was now in operation. And not surprisingly, Cinderella's stepsisters were two of the leading protagonists.

Perhaps Cinderella and the prince did eventually find each other again. Left without any of the trappings of power or artifice, they might have discovered each other as real human beings. It was rumoured at one stage that Cinderella was taking a night degree at university, while the prince grew vegetables and babysat back at their cottage. But nobody really knows for sure ...

Linda Kavanagh

The Soothsayer's Quest

ONCE UPON A time in the ancient land of Éirinn lived a witty woman called Mary Rose Regina. No ordinary woman was this, for she was of the blood of the old fairy folk and so possessed a wisdom beyond her years. Her father was a convert to the new Christian religion. He had named her after their queen of heaven. Her mother believed in the old ways. She had implored the goddesses to guide her and insisted that Mary study long and hard under the tutelage of the wise women, the midwives and healers, until she was imbued with knowledge of herbal remedies and potions for every ailment. So it came to pass that her fame had reached the farthest hill in her native province when Ruairi the druid came her way.

Now it happened that the queen of the land wished to employ a soothsayer, a person learned in medicine and music, wise in the ways of the world and with a knowledge of the Brehon Laws. She had despatched Ruairi to search the length and breadth of Éirinn in the hope of finding such a rare creature.

Mary stood before him tall and proud. He questioned her from dawn to dusk and declared there was but one flaw in her education.

'But let you spend the next seven years with me learning the Law and all will be well,' he said. 'You are no stranger to hard graft and you will be richly rewarded. Do you consent?'

'I do,' said Mary, knowing that success would mean attaining the highest office in the land.

On that same day, in an eastern province, the king's nephew, Lenny, declared himself a contender for the position of soothsayer, in opposition to the druid's choice. This had never happened before. When Ruairi returned it was all he could do to contain his fury at the king for allowing such a scandal. Ruairi knew that Lenny the knave had risen to prominence through trickery. A genial, likeable fellow, he was nevertheless a crafty double dealer. The King was weak willed. He owed a favour to his brother who had lent him ships and men on his last sortie across the water. He had agreed in haste. The druid was unable to disallow the contest but he succeeded in postponing the final choice for four years, when the queen would return from her long voyage east.

Ruairi set about his tutoring with determination. How to fit seven years learning into four was a daunting task, but this wench was a willing pupil and learned eagerly. Together they would attempt the impossible.

On the queen's return the contest was announced. It consisted of a quest for the fifth province. Whosoever returned with a jewel from this legendary land would be declared the true soothsayer. A sojourn of seven moons was allowed to accomplish the feat.

Lenny the Knave first attempted to discover the location of the famed province by bribing sea captains. Then he hired mercenaries to search the rivers and glens in the remotest parts of the land and promised his weight in gold to the first man who returned with a jewel.

Mary repaired to her native western province, to the wild hills and windy valleys to reflect on the meaning of the quest and to consider the wisest course of action. She fasted and prayed for guidance, listening to the wisdom of wind and sea and consulting oracles. On the seventh day a maiden appeared to her in a vision. 'I am your spirit guide,' she declared, 'sent to you from the goddess Bríd. You must journey alone to the far north and forge a bond of friendship with the sons of Uladh, enemies of your people. This bond of friendship is the jewel of great price which you must carry home.'
In an instant she vanished.

Mary set off without a word. For six moons she travelled north, enduring many hardships. When finally she came to the court of Uladh there was such fuss and commotion that her presence was hardly noticed. The queen was in the birthing chamber and had just given birth. Mary was about to present herself to the druidic priestesses when the midwife came into the hallway, beating her breast in anguish: the child, the king's firstborn heir was about to die.
Mary acted swiftly. From her pouch she produced a healing balm to soothe the mother, then attended to the birth. The chord had almost strangled the child. Deftly she loosened the sinewy knot and the babe gasped. The midwife fell at her feet, giving thanks and praising her skill.
The king made a pledge to this illustrious stranger: a gift of the brightest jewel in his crown or any

manner of gift she might desire. But he was aghast at her answer. 'A bond of friendship between my people and your people, enemies of old. Let me take back the royal shield with the red hand as proof of our pact.' The northern king was a man of honour. 'Let it be so, from this day forth', he pronounced. Mary was given a bronze chariot, horses with jewelled livery and the king's escort to ensure her safe passage home.

Lenny the knave had begun feasting in anticipation of his triumph as the day of the seventh moon drew near. Nowhere in the known world, from the Shannon to the Nile, did there exist a pearl of such great price as he now possessed.

But as Mary's entourage reached the plains of Meath, word came to him of the hordes that accompanied her. She had found some great prize to be sure. But what could it be? He gathered his spies and sent them to greet her dressed as minstrels. Secretly they planned to steal or destroy whatever gem she had found. But they returned empty-handed, saying only that some great treasure was hidden in a casket and travelled under guard.

Lenny fumed at their incompetence. He plotted with his father who persuaded the king to add one further trial to the contest. Before presenting the jewel from the fifth province they must compose a lay, honouring the druid who had served as soothsayer for many years. A soothsayer who was also a bard would be highly favoured. The king agreed, not knowing that Lenny would prepare his poem in advance while Mary would have to compose hers on the spot. In this way the knave acquired an unfair advantage.

At moonrise they both entered the castle. The queen, the druid, the king and his brother were all assembled along with their cohorts and messengers. A great feast had been prepared for the victor.

Lenny sallied into the chamber with great trumpet playing and loud drumming. He bowed to Ruairi and began to recite:

> Ruairi the Brave, Ruairi the kind,
> A soothsayer of uncommon mind.
> A wiser judge, nor a truer friend,
> Will ne'er be found in all the land.

He appeared to falter, performed another verse, then presented his pearl in a jewelled case, reciting another poem extolling the virtues of the queen and the pearl, comparing their worth. Eventually he bowed and smiled.

The king invited Mary Rose Regina to reply. Ruairi raised his voice, objecting angrily. A furore ensued and the queen rose to still the tumult. But there was no need, for Mary had accepted the challenge. A hush fell over the gathering. She began:

> Ruairi the seer is indeed brave,
> And none can say he is not kind.
> But neither bard nor poet is our Lenny,
> I wager he did spend a penny,
> To hire a quill for good or ill,
> To regale us ere we swill our fill.
> Yet I salute our seer, Ruairi mo chroí,
> who has kept our land peaceful and free.

Before a cheer could rise she brandished the shield and laid it at the feet of the queen.

'The fifth province', she declared, 'is the province of the heart. This red hand of friendship will ensure peace and prosperity throughout all the land for seven generations. This is the jewel I present.'

The Queen stepped forth. 'Leonard you have done well,' she intoned, 'and we are most pleased with your efforts, but Mary, you have indeed excelled. I pronounce you soothsayer!'

A roar of acclamation thundered through the castle. There followed much feasting and rejoicing. Invitations were sent to the northern rulers who gladly accepted. Ambassadors from far and near joined in the celebrations.

Mary's reputation for wisdom and fair dealing became a legend. And so it was recorded in the annals of the masters that no soothsayer ever matched her from that day to this.

Joni Crone

Red Riding Hood

In my scarlet patched-together coat
I built a cage of teeth of rusty tin.
I fitted seven locks with ancient numbers -
forgot the numbers - clambered in.
My cloak had once been bitten from my body
by a wolf-grandmother, old and wild.
But I was never to speak of it.
I was only a child.
It was my secret with granny,
the only one who knew,
and the wood filled up with snarls
between us as I grew.
Now she prowls with eyes and ears
larger than she can use. She lingers.
She thrusts cold claws at me through bars,
they become warm fingers.
She wants to mend my riding hood
but I'm wrapped in it against her pleas;
I know a woman from a wolf
but I suspect apologies.
My hood and I are safer in my cage
whatever meanings she may bring.
A grandmother is not a wolf
but stories can be anything.

Zoë Fairbairns

Alice in Thunderland

Prologue

In earlier editions of *Fairytales for Feminists*, we
followed Alice's adventures in the strange place
called Thunderland. There a fembly is a female who
might speak only during chatter time, and a membly
is a male who dominates the world around him. In
Chapter Three, we learned how Alice had witnessed a
mismatch in Thunderland. The result of the
mismatch, apart from the sad shrinkage and defeat of
the fembly and the unnatural bloating of the membly,
was a tiny new wembly. Because no one seemed to
wish to be responsible for this half-formed creature,
Alice picked it up and put it in her pocket and
followed the crowd out of the clearing.

Chapter Four

It seemed that all were making for a giant-sized
building. Alice had never seen a building which
reached so high that she had to crane her neck to look
at the top of it, or indeed to look at the azure about it.
She missed her friend the fembly because she might
have told her the purpose of this building and the
reason for its size. In Harmony Land, which was
Alice's native country, no building was allowed to
predominate over the contours of the land or the
height of the inhabitants. In Harmony Land, and
Alice sighed to remember it, everything worked in

relation to everything else. Actions have consequences. Words have echoes. Thoughts penetrate mountains. Ripples in the pond make storms in the ocean. These were part of the credo of Harmonisers. Yet here in Thunderland each set of actions seemed to have its own value and its own set of rules without being in any way interlinked. Except, thought Alice, for one interconnection. The femblies always come out the losers although they themselves did not seem to believe so. And after Alice had witnessed the mismatch and seen the bloated condition of the membly she began to wonder if some memblies were not also losers, in fact if not in theory.

The road to the building had been long and rocky. On the way there were many potholes and even chasms. To Alice's horror several of the fembly creatures, especially those who travelled in groups, fell into these chasms and were lost forever. Some howled loudly as they fell down and threw fragments of their clothes or pieces of paper with strange words scrawled on them up to their comrades. The braver among the femblies reached for these remnants and passed them on to each other secretly. Once or twice a membly caught hold of one and he either read it and tore it up in contempt or burst out laughing and passed it around to his group. Sometimes he passed a fragment to femblies with much shaking of his head and waving of his stick and the femblies then laughed dutifully. Some of the memblies went so far as to try to push a few femblies into the potholes, and for all Alice could see might have succeeded in pushing one or two into the chasms.

By this time Alice noticed a change in herself which worried her but about which she could do little. She was beginning to shrink. Either that or she was being pressed deeper into the ground beneath her. It was an unfamiliar experience and she had not yet learned to find a coping mechanism for it. She murmured the ritual prayer she had learned as a child from her grandmother, who had learned it from *her* grandmother, and so on back through the generations. It was the emergency prayer; 'I am who am. I am the imperishable. I am the impregnable I. I am the creator and giver of life. I am the one.' To her relief as she chanted it she stopped shrinking. But she had already lost a few inches and she determined that as soon as she escaped from this crowd, which had by this time grown hugely, she would concentrate on regaining height. The strange thing was that, as Alice had shrunk, the little wembly creature in her pocket had grown and at one stage, as Alice stumbled over a pothole, actually fell out of her pocked with a screech of annoyance.

'Mamba,' the creature said, 'you are leading me the wrong way.'

'I'm not leading you at all,' said Alice. 'I'm just giving you a ride so that you can get safely to wherever you want to go.'

'You're my mamba,' said this creature, who only a short while ago had been a bright little pair of eyes and a plaintive voice. 'If things go wrong for me, it's your fault.'

'My fault!' Alice exclaimed. 'I do my best for you. I carry you in my pocket this long journey. What is my fault?'

'I didn't ask to be born,' said the creature importantly. Alice burst out laughing at the impudence of it and everyone around looked at her in annoyance.

By this time the crowd had reached the front door of the building. This was an ugly, iron-framed affair with memblies' heads carved on it. In the forecourt were sculpted statues of memblies on horses or standing on plinths with their arms raised, or holding writing tablets. There were hundreds of them. As Alice was pushed through she felt a hand reach for hers and turning around saw to her great relief that it was her fembly friend.

'Isn't it exciting?' the fembly said. 'At long last. To think I have lived to see this day!'

It was an odd thing to say, Alice thought, because the fembly had quite obviously not lived very long. However, Alice's need for information was great.

'Why are there no fembly statues?' she asked.

'Oh, but there are,' said the fembly proudly. 'Look!' and she pointed to a corner where a sad-looking statue holding a membly baby stood in an archway covered with plants. 'There is the She who represents us all.'

'Yes,' said Alice. 'But she doesn't look like you. Is she like you? Was she one of you? Will your statue be in the forecourt some day?'

'I don't do important things,' said the fembly. 'Femblies never do important things. Only people who do important things have their statues in the forecourt.'

'What are important things?' Alice asked.

'You are very stupid,' the fembly said angrily. 'And I warned you about asking too many questions. Lucky for you everyone is so busy today they are not being picked up. Otherwise you'd be for it, let me tell you.'

At that precise moment a gong sounded. Over the front door a brightly coloured platform unfolded and on to it stepped a membly wearing a shiny coat with lots of brass objects on it and lots of coloured ribbons.

'Who is he?' Alice asked.

A membly beside her gave her a very dirty look and hissed, 'Keep quiet. He is the Hero Boss. He will guide us into the right path and bless our righteousness. For we are the chosen ones. We who follow our hero have moved on to the right path and travel to our destiny.'

'It was a very potholey path,' said Alice, 'and full of chasms. There were many accidents on the way.'

'There are always a few mishaps,' said the membly. 'You have to accept those. Look at all the buttons on our Hero Boss. He has had to push many into chasms, though his heart broke to do it, so that he could lead us to our destiny.'

'He had better not try to push me into a chasm,' said Alice, 'or he'll get what for.'

The membly's attention was distracted by the appearance of another creature, a fembly who was ushered out by various attendants and who stood beside the Hero Boss looking a little bewildered but smiling. At the sight of her all the femblies started cheering and the memblies scratched their little polls in confusion and then the Hero Boss cheered so they all cheered too. Everyone cheered like mad. Alice thought this was great fun and she joined in the cheering.

'This is a great day,' the fembly said. 'This is the greatest day of my life.' Alice could not but be glad for her but she thought she could not have had many great days if journeying on such a terrible road and losing so many of her friends to stand cheering in front of a big building with a coloured platform was a great day.

'She has made it to the platform,' the fembly said. 'She will have a say.'

'I should hope so,' thought Alice although she did not say it aloud because she had already had a few dirty looks and was afraid of shrinking more. Added to that the mamba creature was by now up to her waist and was actually trying to climb up on to her back for a better view.

'Please get off my back,' Alice said politely.

'I will not,' said the mamba. 'Your back is my ladder and up it I will climb.'

'You'd better let it climb,' said the fembly, 'or you'll get an attack of the guilts. Terrible cramps. You can be in bed for weeks with them.'

To Alice's horror, the little mamba had already succeeded in climbing half way up her back and was clinging on to her for dear life. Alice wriggled and squirmed and tried to shake her off for she found her weight oppressive and painful. She hadn't minded carrying the creature in her pocket. In fact for a while it had been quite pleasant and in an odd way comforting. There were moments on that journey to this place when Alice had experienced what she realised was the Thunderland sensation of loneliness. The membly creature for a while alleviated this loneliness. But halfway up her back, and heading fast

for her shoulders - that was going too far. She reached
one arm behind her back to grasp the creature's legs.
Imagine her outrage when her so-called friend gave
her a whack on the arm and said, 'None of that.
You've got to do your duty. We all had to do it.' 'What
has that got to do with anything?' asked Alice. 'What
you do is your business. What I do is mine.'

'You've got a thing or to two learn,' said the
fembly. 'And the sooner you learn it the better. You
have to learn to shape up or formcon. We started very
young. It will be much harder for you but I'll help
you.'

'No,' said Alice. 'Please do not. It sounds extremely
painful and I do not wish to form con.'

'Like it or not,' said the fembly, 'you'll learn.'

Alice noticed with some bewilderment that the closer
they were to the building the more arrogant the
fembly became. Where was the clingy pathetic
creature who had wept such tears at their first
meeting? Where was the little spark of something,
something, something? Alice could not quite think
what, but it was something. And then Alice realised
that for the first time since she came to Thunderland
she had forgotten what she was going to think.

The mamba was climbing on to her neck and had
stretched her little paw up to Alice's head. Alice put
her own hand up to push it back and she felt, just
about her ears, a few feathers. She pulled one out and
she remembered the story about the femblies growing
feathers instead of brains. She looked around to see if
anyone was staring at her but no one noticed. Instead
everyone was staring intently at the fembly on the
platform. What would she do or say, Alice wondered.

What could she do or say with the Boss Hero standing so close to her with all his brass buttons! Perhaps she will sing a song, Alice thought hopefully, or do a somersault or show them all how to fly. It will be really good, Alice thought. And if she does something really good I am quite sure my feathers will stop growing and my memory will come back. What was the word I wanted? What was the word? What was the word?

And then she remembered. Spirit. The fembly, even in her tears, had spirit. But before she had time to consider the change in her friend the fembly on the platform began to speak. As she opened her mouth all the memblies clustered around, looking terribly solemn.

'We will begin again,' said the fembly. 'Let us begin again.'

It did not seem to Alice to be a particularly significant remark and yet it was greeted with something amounting to awe. Beside Alice her fembly friend said with satisfaction. 'You see. It was worth coming this far.'

The Boss Hero then opened his mouth. 'This is a great day,' he said. 'The fembly has had a new hair-do. She has a new skirt. The fembly looks good. I salute the fembly.' And everyone started cheering again. At this point the mamba managed to reach Alice's head; she pulled herself up by the feathers which were growing rampantly on poor Alice's head and joined in the cheering. Alice could feel herself sinking, sinking into the ground, being pressed down deeper and deeper. As she was going down and mamba leaped off her head, shouted 'Thanks for the ride, sucker,' and vanished into the crowd.

.

Alice felt another sensation now. Not loneliness. She had identified that one. It was like loneliness. Akin to loneliness. It was loss. A loss sensation. What was this loss sensation? It was the grief most feared in Harmony Land and Alice groaned as she realised that she had come to face it. She was suffering the terrible disease of alienation. And as she lay, trampled into the mud, while all around her everyone cheered and jumped for joy, she noticed that the feathers were beginning to fall out of her head. Well, she thought, out of every evil may come good. My attack of alienation is rotting my feathers. Good, thought Alice. Very good. I'll get out of this mess yet.

Will she?

Maeve Kelly

No More Embroidery

A LOUD WAIL rent the chorus of maidensong in the Garden of Lugh and echoed off the nearby mountain tops. The daughters of Bregia looked up from their needlework. Fiall was having difficulty fashioning the stitches Emer had taught her; she persisted in putting the gold thread where the silver should be, and the silver where the gold should go. Fiall was miserable. She regretted ever having come to this place.

At that time in Ireland marriage was the only occupation open to maidens. In order to acquire a husband, a maiden had to possess six gifts or virtues: the gift of wisdom, the gift of chastity, the gift of embroidery, the gift of beauty, the gift of voice and the gift of sweet speech. Emer, daughter of Forgall Manach, the wily, not only possessed these gifts, she excelled at all six; and maidens who were lacking in virtue were sent to spend some time with her so that they might acquire her skills, through practice and observation. Fiall was one such maiden.

When Emer and her students were not discussing their marriage prospects, they broke into song and the sweet sound of their voices filled the air. Fiall found she could not join in their chorus.

Her older sister had last year divorced her husband; she had collected together her dowry and returned home. Fiall knew too much and she was concerned about the fate that lay in store for her.

Fiall's great love was horses but she was seldom given the opportunity to ride Lúidín, her favourite black stallion, except when the entire household would go together to the great gatherings at Teamhair to celebrate the Feasts of Bealtaine and Lúghnasa. During the long months between these two events, Emer, Fiall, and the other maidens were confined to the Grianán, the sunny chamber of the house which had been allocated to them.

On this particular day, they had moved outside to the small garden where the flowers and herbs, used in the making of unguents, were in full bloom. Forgall Manach had left early to do some fishing in Connacht. Aoife and Eithne, two of the daughters of Bregia, sensing Fiall's despair, tired to comfort her and she, in turn, confided in them.

At this time, unknown to the maidens, two youths were on their way to visit them: Cúchulainn, the boy upstart from Ulster, and Laeg, his charioteer, who wasn't much better. Cúchulainn had just grown out of his boyhood and all the men in the court of his uncle, Conchobar, king of Ulster, had had enough of his smart-ass feats and his pretty face. They were plagued by their wives and daughters who had eyes only for the boy-wonder and they demanded that a wife be found for him immediately.

Cúchulainn was not easily pleased. None of the maidens procured by the court was good enough. Once at Teamhair he had glimpsed Emer of the golden hair and the six great gifts. None other would satisfy him.

Once again that day the maidensong was interrupted, this time by the clatter of hooves and the clanking of a chariot. The maidens laid aside their embroidery. Had Forgall returned so soon? Were the salmon not biting? Even as they thought to see his dour figure come storming over the drawbridge, a tall blonde youth vaulted into their presence. He was followed by a shorter, ruddier one.

Cúchulainn's crimson five-folded tunic was familiar, as was the white hooded shirt embroidered in red gold. The daughters of Bregia had seen him prancing around at Teamhair. They recognised the fine needlework, the northern motifs.

He came to the point immediately. Any other maiden would have panicked when she heard what he had to say, but not Emer. She drew on her gift of wisdom and began speaking in riddles, but he was able to match her, word for word. Then, in order to give herself time to think, she demanded that he perform some impossible feats which would keep him occupied for a few years.

As Cúchulainn was propositioning Emer, Laeg made overtures to Fiall but she teased him and tricked him also. Then thinking they had performed a good day's work, the two boyos departed as suddenly as they had come.

There was consternation in their wake. Some of the maidens thought Emer the luckiest girl on earth to be courted by so fine a youth in so finely embroidered a shirt. Fiall, Aoife and Eithne were not impressed. They stated their case:

'Who does that young upstart from the north, that goes around killing people for a living, think he is?'

'Did you hear about the day he took up arms? When he came back to the court with his chariot full of bleeding heads, he was in such a frenzy that they had to send out three times fifty women, and they stark naked, in order to calm him?'

'How could you marry a complete stranger, and he as wild as that?'

'We all have to marry complete strangers,' chirped the other maidens. Fiall, Aoife and Eithne continued:

'Think of what you will have to go through before you marry him.'

'You have been practising chastity all these years. For what end? Don't you know that Conchobar has the first forcing of all maidens in Ulster? If you choose to marry the nephew, you must sleep with the uncle first, and we all know what a dirty old man Conchobar is.'

'Remember what he did to Deirdre.'

'The first forcing is only the beginning. You know what happens next - babies. Have any of you ever seen a baby being born?'

They shook their heads. The trio were enjoying themselves now:

'That's because babies are born out in the woods, in the dead of night, winter and summer.'

'And if the baby's head hits a stone, that's deemed an omen of good luck.'

As soon as the baby's born, he's given away to strangers to be reared.'

That swung it.

The following morning Emer called the maidens together. She again exercised her gift of wisdom. There were sighs and gasps as she spoke. Never before had such words been uttered in any grianán.

Never before had maidens considered the alternative options open to them.

A week later, as the feat of Lúghnasa dawned, a great cortege of chariots left the Garden of Lugh. Forgall and his cohorts rode at the head of the procession. The maidens occupied the chariots to the rear. Fiall and Aoife rode their stallions, keeping an eye on the spare horses they had tethered to the chariots.

When they had crossed the great Plain of Bregia, the cortege came to a halt at the washing place of the Horses of Dea and, while the men and their mounts were being watered, Fiall carefully unhooked the spare horses.

The maidens mounted swiftly and Fiall led them through a secret passage that lay between the Great Vat and the Little Vat.

Seeing what was afoot, Fedelm, the Great Sí Woman of Rath Cairn, brought down a heavy mist which covered the whole of Bregia, so that the men could not see to follow them. And when Emer and Fiall and the others had crossed the Back of the Great Sow, they came to a valley where the land was fertile and there was pasture in abundance. It was here they settled.

Later that night they lit a great fire and threw all their embroidered clothes on to it. Then they wove some practical cloth. As the years passed, they bred horses and their stables became famous.

Once a year, on the Feast of Samhain, they invited men into their home to add to their enjoyment of the celebration. And always on the following morning,

Fedelm wove a great web of forgetfulness over them
before they were released back into the world.

Celia de Fréine

Snow White

WHEN I MARRIED Max, it was like a dream come true. I was in love with him. He was, still is, a fabulously wealthy man and we live in a vast and gorgeous house in a part of the country I adore. My life as a bank clerk before I met him was unpromising but I regret to say the new life hasn't really lived up to all my expectations. Material wealth isn't all it's cracked up to be. I hardly ever see my husband. He always seems to be away on business trips. I run the house and estate as best I can, having to live with the legacy of how capable his dead wife was. But worst of all I have to try and make Snow White, my sullen, suspicious step-daughter, happy.

Perhaps I am being unkind. She has had a tough time of it. Her adored mother died when Snow White was seven. For the last nine years she has been her father's favourite and now she has me to contend with as a rival (at least she would if her father was ever here). She has no friends. Her every whim is catered for. She is frustrated, lonely and spoilt. She has a lively imagination though and reads a lot. She has read that all step-mothers are evil, cruel and generally nasty.

Snow White has a lovely figure. I bought her a present of an Azzedine Alaia dress a short time ago to show it off - trying to buy her affection to a certain extent. She said she was too fat for it. I persuaded her to try it on. She said it was far too tight. Then she couldn't get the damn thing off and accused me of trying to asphyxiate her. Since then she has been eating hardly anything and I'm worried about her. She will eat only fruit and vegetables that she herself has prepared. I've been nagging her a little about it which has only increased her resentment towards me.

I offered her an apple the other day, a rather beautiful, red, rosy apple with a lovely bouquet that I had picked in the orchard specially for her. She said she would choke on it, that anything I touched turned to poison. Then she flounced off. I began to eat the apple myself. I reached the core after a few bites and found there was a worm in it. I threw the rest away.

. . . . . .

Snow White has decided to move out of home. Her father is away and there is nothing I can do about it. She's joining some sort of commune deep in the forest. She wants to be as close to nature and as far away from me as possible. I tried to reason with her. She called me an evil witch who had driven her father away and turned him against her. I began to help her pack.

I feel very isolated. I have lost touch with all the people I used to know, all the people at the bank. I have started talking to the furniture but it's like talking to a block of wood. I get the most satisfaction out of my mirror even though it just reflects my own opinions. I consulted it about Snow White, told it how I had decided to wash my hands of her, had resolved to have nothing more to do with her. I asked the mirror if it thought I was being too harsh. I was reminded that I too had been awkward and rebellious when I was young, that Snow White was ill-prepared for the real world after living in the rarified atmosphere of her palatial home, and that we were both alone and were really each other's only allies. So I asked the woodchopper, a nice young man who often goes into the forest, if he could keep an eye on her for me. He said it would be and honour and a privilege. I think he might have a bit of a soft spot for her.

. . . . . .

I've been experimenting with apples, making cider. It's rather good. Seán, the woodsman, has been taking it down to the village for me and selling it. I've come up with my own unique recipe; the worms in the apples seem to enhance the flavour! Whenever we meet, Seán gives me bulletins on Snow White's progress. Apparently she has been getting a little fed up with her new lifestyle. She is being used as a skivvy by the other members of the commune who take advantage of her guilt about her privileged background. Also the tiny cottage is very cramped and overrun with wildlife who leave droppings everywhere that she has to clear up.

Some prince who is interested in photography has been hanging around taking pictures of her, telling her that she should be a model and there are rumours of romance in the air. I won't try to influence her either way but I know where romances with royalty can lead to if you're the right sort of girl and I think she is far too young for marriage. Still, I know she wouldn't listen to anything I might have to say on the subject.

. . . . . .

Snow White is home again. She married the prince. She left the prince. She says he was only interested in her as an object or photographic image. She has made some new friends through her royal connections - Cinderella and Rosebud (or the Sleeping Beauty as she is popularly known, a bit of a dozey girl really). Of the two Snow White is closer to Cinderella. They have so much in common. They both married into royalty, have husbands who treat them like clothes horses, and of course they both have wicked step-mothers. Cinders says she just can't take the strain anymore. Everytime she goes to a ball or social occasion she is expected to wear a gown more fabulous than the last.

The three princesses have formed a society called the SPVF, the Society for the Protection of Victims of Fantasy. Their first recruit has been a nervous little girl called Red Riding Hood who drives everywhere in a taxi. She always seems to be passing personal remarks about people's appearances, like 'her nose is too long,' or 'he has such pale skin.'

Snow White and I are getting along better now. We've reached a truce, but this lady-of-the-manor-with-absentee-lord routine doesn't really suit me. Also I actually have been a little wicked lately. Remember Seán the woodsman whomc I thought had a soft spot for Snow White? Well, it turned out I got it slightly wrong and we've been getting along like a house on fire. Little Red Riding Hood isn't the only scarlet woman around here.

Róisín Sheerin

After Reading The Swan Prince

It was dark for her, sitting at the edge
of a dim lake,
waiting for the beat of great wings,
hearing only the magpies' chuck,
the sedge hissing.

But it was no more unlikely that the sky's rim
should curdle, glint,
throb towards her, bearing the prince's token
than that this toadface telephone beside my bed
should ring,
and I be woken from long sleep
by your voice, long missing.

Roz Cowman

The King, the Queen and the Donkey Man

ONCE UPON A time, the king and queen of the fairies made their home in a forest near the city of Athens in Greece. The king was named Oberon, and the queen, Titania; and both were very fond of doing what they pleased. Titania passed her days among the courtiers, a charming crowd of dainty fairies, who danced, told stories and tended the flowers that grew in the forest. Oberon, who regarded such pastimes as unmanly, escaped whenever he could with his pal, Puck, a renegade fairy and master prankster. Together, in the darkest leafy glades of the forest, Oberon and his sidekick would knock back quantities of fermented berry juice, and exchange wisecracks, which kept them amused for hours.

In the evenings, Oberon fluttered home, where the little fairies stuffed him full of blackberries, figs, and the honey bags from bumble-bees. Later, Titania massaged Oberon's back, while briefing him on the latest news of their fairy kingdom. As he drifted off to sleep, Oberon marvelled at how well this lifestyle suited him.

Indeed, things were going along swimmingly until the day that Titania was made guardian to a bouncing boy-child. Baby William was a lively human infant, with pink cheeks and yellow hair, and as different from the insubstantial fairies as chalk is from cheese. The queen was devoted to him; and Oberon watched jealously as Titania played peepo with the boy, and sang to him ancient fairy songs.

The fact was that Oberon desired the child for himself. He wanted the boy to walk in his own footsteps. He yearned to teach William all he knew: how to hunt for plover or squirrels in the forest; how to steal the finest feathers from a peacock; how to carve spears out of the best white oak. So, Oberon approached his queen with the confident, cocksure step of a king who generally gets his own way.

'The child is mine,' Oberon purred.

Titania stared him down with steely eyes. 'No way!' she said, folding her glittering wings around William.

Oberon was taken aback. He had not anticipated any failure to co-operate. 'I said, give me the boy,' he insisted, astonished to hear a titter from one of the fairy courtiers, who were all listening goggle-eyed.

'Over my dead body,' Titania smiled, and blew a kiss across the distance between them, much as if she were tossing in bandages after a hand grenade.

Shouting for Puck, the fairy king slouched off, his handsome face livid, and his mind dwelling upon revenge.

As it happened, there was a group of Athenian workers rehearsing a play in the forest. These workers were the salt of the earth - a carpenter, a cobbler, a miller, a weaver, and a tailor - all hard-working men who earned their bread through the use of their hands and the sweat of their brows. They were determined to make a success of their little play, even though they were unaccustomed to using big words and enacting strong emotions.

As Oberon and Puck flew through the forest, they chanced upon this rehearsal. Being quite invisible themselves, they decided to watch. In no time at all, they were roaring with laughter at the simple antics of the unsophisticated players.

'Who is that oaf playing the leading man?' Oberon inquired.

'He is Bottom, the weaver,' replied Puck.

'Then he's aptly named, for he is, indeed, the bottom of the heap!' Both the fairy king and his sidekick howled raucously, as if this witticism were very funny indeed.

His spirits revived, Oberon settled upon a plan to put Titania in her place. 'Why not make the fairy queen fall in love with this baboon, Bottom?' he murmured in a silky voice.

'Hah!' snorted Puck, 'That would be revenge indeed. Only who could fall in love with such a bumpkin?'

'Look,' whispered Oberon. From the fob pocket in his waistcoat, the fairy king withdrew a tiny vial. 'Love-in-idleness! The juice of a pansy flower, impaled by Cupid's arrow. One drop on Titania's sleeping eyelids, and she will dote madly upon the next creature she sees.'

'Brilliant!' Puck was aquiver with excitement. 'But may I suggest a refinement?'

'By all means.'

'Give Bottom the head of a donkey, so then your queen might truly love an ass!'

'How perfectly vile!' Oberon agreed.

And so it came to pass that when Titania woke from her sleep, she fell madly in love with the weaver, Bottom, who had the body of a man, but the head of a donkey.

The spectacle of the lovely fairy queen in the arms of a donkey-man caused Oberon to slap his thigh with joy. 'Just listen to him talk,' Oberon sneered. 'He brays!'

Titania was too much in love to care. And Bottom was in love with Titania. In the evenings, the donkey-man sprinkled buds of musk-roses on to her bed, and wove violets into her golden hair. In the mornings, he made himself useful about the palace, weaving, market gardening, and playing on the pipes, so that the fairy courtiers might have music for their dancing. He was also good with Baby William. Together, the fairy queen and her lover played chase with the child, and Bottom was always ready to soothe away tears with a gentle nuzzle, or even to change a nappy, when the need arose.

Soon Oberon got bored with the sight of his mistress canoodling with a donkey, so he applied the antidote to Titania's eyes. He stepped back to enjoy the fun. With relish, he anticipated Titania's shriek at the sight of her lover's bristles and snout.

But it never came. The fairy queen failed to leap for protection into Oberon's waiting arms. On the contrary, she studied Bottom's rough features closely, and saw that they were shining with the goodness of his soul. The fact is that the donkey-man's kindness had made such an impression upon Titania's heart, that she loved him truly, no matter what he looked like.

Of course the restoration of her senses also made Titania understand the game that Oberon had been playing.

'What a nasty mocking mind you have,' she complained. 'Only a louse could cook up a scheme like that!'

'Now, now,' Oberon said sheepishly.

'Just keep your silly mouth shut,' Titania said. 'There are some things you shouldn't mock, and love is one of them.'

So, with no more ado, Titania told Oberon to pack his bags and leave the forest. And that is what he did. Then Titania, the queen of the fairies, lived happily ever after with her new partner, Bottom, and the bouncing boy-child, William.

Ivy Bannister

Happy Ever After and Other Obsessions

ONCE UPON A time there was a little girl who was born with a head of thick fair hair. It seemed at the time to be the only propitious circumstance around, for giant question marks stood over her future. One morning however, a tall dark woman in black spotted her in her orphanage cot, and brought her home to a Martello tower in the country. We are going to live happily ever, after she crooned.

Nobody quite knew how she squared it with the adoption workers, and people in the village talked as people do. Some said the dark woman was really the child's grandmother; others said there must be some nasty secret lurking in that old tower. One old man said that the herbs she grew on the balcony were poisonous. The dark woman would never let anyone past the front door. She spent a lot of time in the round room at the top of the tower painting, and little Rapunzel - for that was the child's name - would paint too. The woman taught Rapunzel that the modern world was corrupt and full of danger, and that they were lucky to live so happily in the country. Television was an instrument of the devil, so Rapunzel was protected from its pernicious influence. Being a contented little girl she made her own amusements. The only difficulty was that she could never see any of the corruption her mother spoke of.

At school, the teacher took her under her wing and she soon had lots of friends in the village.

Once the teacher had sent a note home suggesting that Rapunzel's hair should be cut. Rapunzel's mother flew into a rage. She said hair was a woman's crowning glory, that cutting it was unnatural. After that the teacher sent no more notes. Rapunzel's plaits grew so long they had to be looped up behind. Rapunzel became adept at filtering school news so it would not upset her mother, and home news so it wouldn't upset the teacher. In this way she moved up through national school taking part in games and pantomimes. She dispensed her mother's herbs and was loved by everyone for her good nature.

When Rapunzel was about twelve, her mother gave up painting and became obsessed with food. Evil persons, she told Rapunzel, were trying to poison the world with additives and preservatives. She decided they would grow their own food. The nearest available land was two miles away, so each morning she would cycle off on an ancient bicycle, her black skirts billowing. At first Rapunzel came along to help, but the language of the neighbouring farmer was so coarse that her mother enjoined her to stay at home. By the time the girl was sixteen, her mother had also become suspicious of the education system, and Rapunzel did her lessons by correspondence. Even then some of the prescribed texts caused problems. Yet, in spite of all, Rapunzel retained her good humour.

Unfortunately, she was also beautiful, and her mother's next virulent obsession concerned men. Men, she told the wide-eyed Rapunzel, were the source of all evil, the reason women did not live happily ever after. When she found her daughter conversing with a neighbour who happened to be male, tall and handsome, Rapunzel's days of freedom ended. She was moved up to her mother's old studio at the top of the tower. Rapunzel's mother was not cruel; the organic vegetable business was doing quite well (in spite of her being choosy about customers), and she installed a rose bathroom and a cooker. When the workmen were finished she blocked the stairs herself, so that the only entrance was from the wooden balcony. Rapunzel fought long and hard to have at least a fire escape but her mother was adamant. A way out is also a way in, she said. In the evening Rapunzel was to let her plaits down over a winch to allow her mother to visit.

At first even Rapunzel's sweet nature was not proof against this trial, and she just sat there not even eating the good organic vegetables. But gradually she recovered and thought of stratagems to make life bearable. Her old teacher smuggled her in books; one friend brought her a rope-ladder so she was occasionally able to escape to the village. Some people talked of informing the guards, but they were afraid of the dark woman who was now openly referred to as the witch. Anyway Rapunzel was hopeful of her mother's latest obsession which concerned the seepage of radon gas. With any luck, Rapunzel thought, we'll remove to a cedarwood bungalow, and all this manoeuvring will be unnecessary. She cut off a foot of her hair and found that her mother didn't notice. Things were definitely looking up.

Then one day Fate came knocking on Rapunzel's tower in the shape of a youngish man in a stylish car.

Rapunzel came out on the balcony with a copy of
Romeo and Juliet in her hand. She thought the man
below could make a passable stab at the part of
Romeo. Another girl might have found him slightly
stooped and lacking in hair, but Rapunzel had had
enough of hair. Even with judicious snipping she still
had several pounds of the stuff hanging around her
and there were her mother's dark wisps as well. The
man had kind eyes, she thought, and his obsession
wasn't of the visible variety. He seemed a better
prospect for happy ever afterhood.

He told her he was a lecturer doing a study of
Martello towers and hers was the most interesting
one he had seen to date. Could he come up and view
it more closely?

'The entry arrangements are a bit weird,' she said.
'Can you climb hair?'

When she let down her yellow plaits, he fell on
them and kissed them passionately (which should
have warned her), then scrambled up.

Once there he proved interesting. Rapunzel's head
whirred with the things he told her and it was all she
could do to expel him before her mother came back
from planting her unadulterated onions. She was
breathing her usual fire and brimstone, averring that
men, particularly organic vegetable sellers, were only
after One Thing.

Rapunzel found no evidence of this in her
relationship with Martin, for such was the young
man's name. He was, it is true, fascinated by her hair,
and liked to sit surrounded by yards of fuzz.
Rapunzel found this rather tiresome but put up with
it for the secondary delights of his visits. One day she
told him about her secret ladder, and suggested she

meet him in the village that evening. Martin was unenthusiastic. He much preferred coming to the tower. It was an oasis of quiet in a mad world, he said. As they sat arms entwined under Rapunzel's sheltering hair, he told her of the problems of academia, the poisoned chalices, the illiterate students. Finally when Rapunzel, who had been reared on fairy stories, was becoming a bit impatient, he asked her to marry him.

'It would be nice to live here,' he said. 'But there's your mother.'

'And the lack of stairs,' Rapunzel added.

He said he would build a miniature tower for her in the city, but in the meantime happily ever after would mean a flat. Rapunzel heaved a sigh of relief and they decided to elope that very night.

That evening her mother seemed slower than ever at climbing the hair. Rapunzel felt guilty about leaving but could not conceal her impatience.

'Oh, hurry up, mother,' she called. But as soon as her mother stood beside her, Rapunzel knew that she knew. Maybe it was telepathy, maybe it was detective work - or maybe she really was a witch.

'You've had a man up here,' her mother spat, and whipping a knife from under her skirt, she sawed off Rapunzel's hair. 'I must protect you until you are able to recognise true happiness,' she said. When she descended she pulled Rapunzel's plaits down after her. Thank heavens she didn't find the rope ladder, Rapunzel thought. I'll just fix my hair and get going.

Rapunzel got to work with her nail scissors and by the time she left the tower, she had as little hair as

Martin himself. He turned pale when she walked into the village pub.

'My God, girl, where is your lovely hair?' he said, his eyes filling with tears.

Rapunzel looked at him for a long moment.

'You mean you only loved me for my hair,' she said.

He turned away and she saw happy ever afterhood going as well.

'I could grow it again,' she offered in sacrificial tones, but just at that moment a dark figure appeared laughing horribly, and threw something into Martin's face. He screamed and Rapunzel ran back to him.

'Slut! harlot!' her mother was shouting. 'You will never live happily ever afterwards!' and she lashed the two of them with Rapunzel's plaits.

Well, it was the most exciting night the village had seen in a long time. Rapunzel's mother was carted off to the asylum, where the quality of the vegetables improved considerably. Poor Martin was rushed to hospital with eye damage. Rapunzel sat beside him in the ambulance and he confessed he was a hair fetishist. She told him it didn't matter; she was into doing good herself and he could have her hair if he needed it.

Rapunzel stayed in the village and dallied with the handsome young neighbour. Then she dallied with the idea of Martin as a smouldering disabled husband *a la* Mr Rochester. She sought him out in the psychotherapist's clinic where he had gone to find himself. The psychotherapist was very interested in Rapunzel, and felt that with her equable nature and her experience of obsessions, she could have a bright future in psychotherapy. Rapunzel rose rapidly in the world of couches and non-direction, while Martin exorcised his experiences with a best-seller called *Hair and Punishment*. The two lived happily together on a provisional basis, with Rapunzel's plaits in a box under the bed.

Máiríde Woods